KARATE KICK

THE **#1**
SPORTS SERIES
FOR KIDS

KARATE KICK

LITTLE, BROWN AND COMPANY
Books for Young Readers
New York   Boston

Little, Brown and Company

Hachette Book Group USA
237 Park Avenue, New York, NY 10017
Visit our Web site at www.lb-kids.com

www.mattchristopher.com

First Edition: July 2009

Library of Congress Cataloging-in-Publication Data

Peters, Stephanie True, 1965–
    Karate kick / [text written by Stephanie Peters. — 1st ed.
        p. cm.
    "Matt Christopher, the #1 sports series for kids."
    Summary: While training for his green belt in karate, Cole Richards
also learns some important lessons about jealousy, competition, respect,
and motivation.
    ISBN 978-0-316-02702-1
    [1. Karate — Fiction.   2. Friendship — Fiction.]   I. Christopher, Matt.
II. Title.
    PZ7.P441833Kar 2009
    [Fic] — dc22

                                                            2008034005

10 9 8 7 6 5 4 3 2 1

Text written by Stephanie Peters

RRD-IN

Printed in the United States of America

KARATE KICK

Ki-ai!"

With a forceful cry, eleven-year-old Cole Richards flipped his best friend Marty Bronson backward over his hip. Marty landed with a thud on the thick floor mat. Cole dropped down and, with a loud "He-*ya!*" aimed a punch at Marty's throat. His fist stopped less than an inch from its target.

They both froze for a moment. Then they relaxed and looked at their martial arts instructor, their sensei.

"Good," said Sensei Joe, nodding.

Cole stood up and adjusted his white gi top so that it lay neatly over the uniform's white pants. He tugged at the ends of the blue canvas belt wrapped around his waist, tightening the belt's knot.

"Okay, Marty, it's your turn," the instructor said. "Cole is going to attack you with one of three grabs —

a single wrist grab, a double wrist grab, or a front choke. When he does, defend yourself."

Marty faced Cole. Cole waited a beat, and then rushed forward and put his hands around his friend's throat.

With a lightning-quick move, Marty flung his arms straight up and outside Cole's arms, fingertips pointed at the ceiling. Then he stepped back, twisted sideways, and dropped one elbow across and down onto Cole's arms.

Cole fell forward and released Marty's neck. Marty delivered two quick elbow jabs at Cole's exposed jaw, punctuating each with energetic cries.

"He-ya! He-ya!"

Those elbow jabs ended the move. The two separated and turned for Sensei Joe's reaction.

"Not bad," he said. "Marty, you attack Cole now."

"Okay!" Marty wrapped his left hand tightly around Cole's right wrist. Cole tried to free himself by pulling his fist up toward his ear with a sharp jerk.

It didn't work.

"Stop," Sensei Joe said. "Cole, what did you do wrong?"

Cole stared at his wrist, still encircled by Marty's fingers, and shook his head, mystified.

"Marty, do you know?" Sensei Joe asked.

"He forgot to turn his wrist first," Marty replied immediately.

"And why would that make a difference?" the instructor prodded.

"Because then the skinniest part of his wrist would face the spot where my thumb and fingers meet," he said. He demonstrated by rotating Cole's wrist. "Without the turn, the widest part of his wrist would be at that spot instead. It's hard for the wide part to force its way through that opening. But it's almost impossible for me to keep my grip on him when the skinny part does."

"Exactly," Sensei Joe said with satisfaction.

A red flush of embarrassment crept up Cole's face. He couldn't believe he'd forgotten such a basic move. It was something he'd learned nearly four years ago, when he'd first started taking karate, for Pete's sake!

"Try again," their instructor said.

This time, when Marty grabbed his wrist, Cole remembered the turn and yanked himself free without a problem.

"Good," Sensei Joe said.

Cole and Marty attacked one another with several

more grabs. Then Sensei Joe told them to join the other students to practice some different defensive moves, called kumites. They bowed to one another and moved from the mats to the main floor of the dojo. Their instructor, meanwhile, disappeared into his office.

Marty nudged Cole. "You know what Sensei Joe's doing, don't you?" he whispered.

Cole glanced through the office windows. "It looks like he's printing something," he said.

"Exactly! And I bet I know what it is!" Marty grinned at him. "It's your invitation to test for your green belt!"

Cole blinked. His mouth grew dry. His heart started thumping in his chest. "My green belt test? You really think so?"

2

Cole had been a karate student for more than four years. Like all beginners, he had started his training in the white belt class. Sensei Joe and the other instructors taught him some basic blocks, kicks, strikes, and stances, plus some simple defensive moves, and how to spar safely against other students. They also taught him his first kata, or series of karate moves.

Each belt level had its own curriculum. After a few months, Cole had learned all the material at the white belt level. But before he could advance to the next rank, yellow belt, he had to demonstrate that he had mastered the white belt skills. That demonstration, or test, was by invitation only and took place on a special day and time outside of class.

Cole had been nervous the day of his first test. But once he began, his anxiety had fled.

For the test, one of his senseis asked him to do some basic moves. Another watched him perform his kata. Finally, Sensei Joe had tested his defensive skills. Cole did each task well and had passed with flying colors. When he accepted his new yellow belt from Sensei Joe at the end of the test, he couldn't stop grinning.

As a yellow belt, Cole learned new moves, a new kata, and practiced all the white belt material as well. In time, he advanced to the next level of orange belt, where he continued to build upon the skills he had learned at white and yellow.

At some karate schools in other parts of the country, green belt followed orange. But at Sensei Joe's dojo, the next level was purple, and then blue, green, and brown. Cole was a blue belt; if he made it through green and brown and continued training, he could eventually achieve the coveted rank of black belt.

That wasn't the end of the road, however. If he wanted, he could train for years to come, for as Sensei Joe often said, there was always something else to learn or some skill to perfect.

To reach blue belt, Cole had gone through the testing experience four times. Each test had been longer and more difficult, for the higher up he climbed, the more he was expected to know. His last test, from purple belt to blue, had lasted more than two hours!

Now, the thought of being invited to test for his green belt filled his stomach with butterflies. There would be so much to remember!

"Hey, boys, shake a leg!"

The call came from Sensei Ann, another instructor. Sensei Ann was a senior in high school but she already had her black belt, a sure sign of her dedication to martial arts. With her warm smile and easy laugh, she was a favorite among the students. She didn't mind joking around with them — but when it was time to train, like now, she was all business.

Cole and Marty quickened their pace. The other students had already formed two lines facing one another. Cole joined one line and Marty took a spot opposite him.

Cole liked pairing with Marty during exercises that required a partner, such as the defensive maneuvers they were about to do. They were the same age, height, and build, and since Marty had just recently advanced to blue belt, they were the same rank, too. While Cole had no problem working with someone shorter or taller or weaker or stronger than he was, he

7

preferred to pair off with someone equal in size, strength, and skill, like Marty.

"Bow to your partner," Sensei Ann called when everyone was ready.

Cole and Marty dipped forward, straightened, and then assumed positions about an arm's length apart.

"Kumite number one," Sensei Ann said. "Marty's side strikes first, the other side defends. Ready? Go!"

Marty lunged forward with a straight-in punch directed at Cole's face.

As the fist neared, Cole burst into action. He slid his left foot back. He twisted his body a quarter turn to the left. He struck out with his right arm, hitting Marty's forearm with the back of his own to push the punch away. Then he flattened and flipped his right hand and thrust the pinky edge at Marty's neck — a strike their instructors called a shuto. That done, he slid his right foot over and twisted back toward Marty, driving the heel of his left hand at Marty's jaw as he did. A split second later, he unleashed a right punch at Marty's midsection.

"Ki-ai!" he shouted with the punch.

"Ye-ow!" Marty yelped in pain. Then he clutched his abdomen and moaned, "Oowww, my gut! *Ooowww!*"

3

For one heart-stopping moment, Cole thought he had really hurt his friend.

But then he realized he couldn't have. After all, he had only touched Marty with his knuckles! If he had actually hit him full force, with that punch or any of his strikes, Sensei Ann would have been on him faster than fleas on a junkyard dog.

So instead of showing concern, he folded his arms over his chest, rolled his eyes, and said, "Nice acting. Are you up for an Academy Award or something?"

Marty straightened, a wide grin on his face. "Just imagining what it'd be like if you really hit me!"

Cole struck a pose, hands circling in front of him. "You better hope you never find out! These bad boys are lethal weapons, you know!"

"Ahem," Sensei Ann interrupted. "Some of us are

trying to practice kumites here. If you'd rather goof off, please step out of line."

The boys stopped clowning around instantly and muttered apologies. At their instructor's command, Cole threw a straight-in punch at Marty. Marty defended himself with the same quick, powerful moves Cole had just used.

When both lines had done the first kumite, Sensei Ann told Marty's side to shift down one spot. Now everybody faced new partners for kumite number two.

Felix, a small boy who had only recently achieved the rank of purple belt, looked up at Cole with trepidation.

"Hey, Felix," Cole greeted him. "What's wrong?"

"I always mess this one up," Felix confessed.

"So don't rush it," Cole suggested. "Do it one step at a time. Then do it again and pick up the pace. Learning to do these kumites right is what this drill is all about, after all!"

"Okay," Felix said, looking a little more cheerful.

Cole came at Felix with a straight-in punch. But unlike the driving punch he'd delivered at Marty, this one was slow and deliberate.

Felix responded with the same twisting arm block used at the start of kumite number one. Then he hesitated.

"Slide your front foot back," Cole coached. "And do the two shutos, right then left, at my neck. Follow those with a right punch to my stomach. Remember?"

"Foot, shuto, shuto, punch," Felix muttered, performing the motions as he said them.

"Good!" Cole praised the other boy. "Now do it all again, with a little more power and speed. Ready?"

This time, Felix didn't hesitate at all. When he finished he gave Cole a big grin. Cole responded with a thumbs-up sign. Then he defended himself against Felix's punch with the same moves. After that, it was time to change partners again.

When Cole saw who he was paired up with next, he almost groaned out loud.

Monique Cleary had started taking karate at the same time as Cole. Back then, she, Marty, and Cole had been good friends; in fact, Cole and Monique had been the ones to convince Marty to join them in learning karate.

But right after he did, something changed. Monique started taking private lessons with Sensei Joe in addition to the regular classes. She also started taking karate much more seriously. She delivered every kick, every strike, and every block as if her life depended upon it! That newfound intensity, plus the extra training, had vaulted her ahead of Cole and Marty. Three months ago, she had earned her green belt.

Cole was more than a little jealous that she was further along in her training than he was. But he could have handled it if not for one thing. Soon after she had reached a higher rank, Monique had started pointing out his smallest errors. It was almost like he was a mouse and she was a cat, waiting to pounce on him!

He knew fellow students were supposed to correct one another when they noticed someone making a mistake. Normally, he didn't mind it; after all, he helped others as much as they helped him. But there was something about the way Monique did it that just drove him nuts.

Now, it was his turn to defend himself against her attack, an uppercut punch, for kumite number three. Monique pushed her curly red hair out of her face and got ready. At Sensei Ann's command, she scooped her right arm up at him.

He twisted sideways and blocked the blow as it rose

toward him. But as he started to do the next moves —
grabbing her wrist and tugging her forward into his
jabbing elbow — he saw Monique's fist continue on its
upward path toward his face!

"Uh-oh," she said smugly, "someone didn't block
very well!"

4

Cole dropped his arms and glared at Monique. "What?"

Sensei Joe appeared behind him. "I believe she said you didn't block very well. And she's right. You rushed the block to get to the elbow strikes. But you'll never get a chance to do the strikes if you don't block first, because her fist will be jammed into your eye. Try it again."

By this time, everyone else was done with the kumite. They all turned to watch Cole and Monique.

Cole flushed from his neck to his scalp as he set up for kumite number three again. This time, when the uppercut came, he struck Monique with as much force as he could muster.

That strike backfired, for a starburst of pain exploded in his own arm. From her gasp, he knew the

14

blow had hurt her, too. But he didn't stop. Instead, he wrapped the fingers of his left hand tightly around her right wrist and, with a quick twisting yank, jerked her into his jabbing right elbow.

Her free hand whipped up to protect her jaw from his jabs.

Cole let go. "I'm not going to hit you!" he said. But secretly, he was glad he had made her think he might. Maybe next time she'd think twice before correcting him!

Sensei Joe and Sensei Ann led the students through several more kumites. They finished just as class time ran out.

"Man, my arm is going to be bruised tomorrow!" Marty said, rubbing the spot where students had struck him over and over. "Everyone's arms are so bony! It's like getting whacked with a broom handle!"

Cole looked at his own forearm and grimaced. "Yeah, my arm is sore, too. But what can you do? Karate is a contact sport, after all!"

"True enough, my friend, and so much more besides," Marty agreed.

They both glanced at the wall where a poster hung. Written on that poster was the basic philosophy of karate as translated from Gichin Funakoshi, the man who had put it forth more than a century earlier: "Seek perfection of character, be faithful, endeavor to do well, respect others, and refrain from violent behavior!"

Sensei Joe clapped his hands then and instructed the students to line up for dismissal. He bowed to them and they returned the courtesy. Then he told them to remove their belts.

Cole widened his stance, loosened the knot, and pulled the belt free. He folded the canvas length neatly, making sure it didn't drag on the floor, and placed it in his right hand. Then he held both hands out in front of him in the ready stance.

His heart started pounding again. If Sensei Joe was going to invite him to test, now was when he'd do it.

Instead, Sensei Joe made an announcement. "Before you go," he said, "I want to tell you about a contest we will be holding here at the dojo."

"What kind of contest?" one of the students asked.

"It's our first annual create-your-own-kata contest," Sensei Joe replied. "Contestants will have until this Sunday to make up a karate routine, their own kata. That afternoon, each student who enters will perform

16

his or her kata for the rest of the class, parents, and other audience members. We will vote for the one we like best and the winner will teach it to us during future classes."

There was an interested murmuring among the students, a sound that stopped immediately when their instructor cleared his throat.

"One final thing," he said. He held out a piece of paper. "Cole, step forward, please."

A jolt of nervous excitement coursed through Cole's body. This was it! That paper had to be his official invitation to test for his green belt!

He was right. "Congratulations," Sensei Joe said, handing Cole the paper.

As the other students applauded, Cole bowed to both of his instructors and shook their hands. Then he returned to the line.

"Told you so!" Marty whispered. "Way to go, buddy!"

"Thanks," Cole replied. "I'm really psyched!"

He was, too. And yet, deep down inside, a worm of doubt wriggled in his gut. What if he made stupid mistakes, like the ones he'd made in class today, during the test? Such mistakes might have been overlooked when he was younger and less experienced. But now? He wasn't so sure his instructors would move him up if he made them.

Sensei Joe interrupted his thoughts. "Okay, everybody, one last question: What's the most important rule in karate?"

It was the same question he asked at the end of every class. The students all knew the answer by heart.

"Never use karate on anybody else unless absolutely necessary!" they responded in unison.

"Exactly!" he said. "You are free to go. If you want to take part in the contest, grab an entry form from my office."

5

Cole and Marty both took contest papers. Cole looked his over as he made his way to the wall of cubbies to collect his socks, shoes, jacket, and gear bag.

"Hey, Marty," he said, "it says here that we can help each other out with the katas. Offer advice, suggestions, that sort of thing. You want to get together tomorrow afternoon and do that?"

Marty nodded. "Sounds good to me. And congrats on your green belt test invite! When's the test, anyway?"

Cole consulted his invitation paper. "Sunday morning, before the contest," he said. He blew out a long breath. Today was Monday; that gave him less than a week to prepare and to make up a kata if he entered the contest. "I just hope I'm ready for the test."

"Ah, you are," Marty reassured him. "But if there's

19

anything you want to practice outside of class, I'll help you."

Cole grinned. "Really?" he said as he put his jacket on.

Marty shrugged. "Sure! In fact, when we get together to work on the kata contest stuff, we can go over your test material, too."

"Thanks, Marty. Even just one extra practice session would really help." He folded his test paper into the contest form and stuck both into his jacket pocket. Then he waited for Marty to finish gathering his belongings so they could walk out together.

Honk, honk! A car pulled into the dojo's parking lot just as they stepped out the door.

"There's my dad," Marty said. "You need a ride today?"

Cole shook his head. "Nah, that's okay, I'm going to walk home on the bike path. See you later!"

"Not if I see you first!" Marty returned as he climbed into the backseat of the car.

Cole laughed and then started walking home.

The bike path had once been railroad tracks. But the trains that used to come through their town had stopped their runs long ago. So the town transformed the tracks into a smooth paved trail that led through wooded areas, past businesses, and behind people's houses.

Both Cole and Marty's houses were on the trail, as was the dojo. Last year, Cole had asked his mother if he could sometimes ride his bike to Marty's house or walk home from karate.

"It's only two miles from the dojo," he'd pointed out, "and just four from Marty's house. I won't be on busy streets. It'll save you gas, too," he'd added persuasively when she hesitated. "Oh, and think of the exercise I'll get!"

She had finally agreed, on one condition. "Come straight home," she'd warned. "Otherwise, I'll be a nervous wreck!"

Cole had laughed off her nervousness. "Mom, nothing's going to happen to me!"

He'd almost added that he knew how to protect himself with karate if someone bothered him. But he decided not to plant that idea in her head; he didn't want to give her any reason to change her mind!

Sometimes, especially on warm summer mornings, the path was crowded with bikers, in-line skaters, joggers, and walkers. But now it was late in the afternoon, cool and cloudy, and the path was deserted.

A stiff breeze rustled the leaves of the trees around him. He shifted his bag of karate equipment higher up on his shoulder and stuck his hands in the pockets of his jacket. His fingers touched the papers he'd put in one. He drew out the contest form and, slowing his pace, began to read through the rules.

CREATE-YOUR-OWN-KATA CONTEST!

The contest is open to all belt levels. Students may help one another if they wish. Each kata should be no less than twelve moves and have at least three strikes, three kicks, and three blocks.

STRIKES: punches, elbows, shutos, palm-heel, spear hand, ridgehand, back fist

KICKS: front snap, side thrust, back, spinning back, roundhouse, knee

BLOCKS: downward, upward, palm, inward, outward, circular outward

STANCES: cat, front, back, and horse

Be sure to use proper stances, change direction, include transition moves—and have fun!

Cole finished reading, folded the paper, and put it back in his pocket. Suddenly, a blur of movement caught his eye. Then he heard a loud cry:

"Look out!"

6

The warning came a second too late. *WHAM!*

A stocky boy on a skateboard crashed into Cole. They fell in a tangled heap onto the hard pavement. The skateboard skittered off into a pricker bush.

Cole groaned, pushed the boy off him, and sat up, shaking his head to clear it.

The boy sat up, too. "Why don't you watch where you're going?" he growled.

Cole stared at the boy — a teenager, he now saw — and retorted, "*You* crashed into *me!*"

The words were barely out of his mouth when he realized that the skateboarder wasn't alone. Leaning against a nearby brick wall were three more teenagers, each holding his own skateboard. Two of them pushed off the wall and ambled toward Cole.

Meanwhile, the first teen had retrieved his board

from the bush. Now he stood in front of the others, looking Cole up and down. His lips turned up in a half-smile, half-sneer.

"Dude," he said, "*what* are you wearing?"

The boys behind him nudged one another and snickered.

At first, Cole thought they were laughing at his jacket. Then he realized they were making fun of his gi. Usually, he wore the karate uniform with pride. But now, confronted by high school kids in torn jeans and T-shirts, he felt a little silly, like he was wearing a costume.

One of the teens, a gangly youth with prominent buckteeth, spoke up. "I know what he's wearing, Darren. It's a karate uniform."

"Ooooo," said the other. "We better watch out. This kid knows karate!" He made a hacking sound and spit a wad of mucus into the bushes.

The third teen, still leaning on the wall, glanced at the spitter with a look of disgust. But he didn't say anything.

"Is that right, kid?" Darren said. "You know karate?"

"I take lessons," Cole said defensively. "So?"

"So," Darren repeated, "let's see what you can do!"

Cole blinked. "What do you mean?"

Darren took a step closer to him and raised his fists. "I mean, let's fight!"

The sudden challenge startled Cole. He licked his lips and tried to swallow, but couldn't.

Then suddenly, the quiet teenager by the wall stepped forward. "Lay off him, Darren," he said. There was a warning in his tone.

"Not a chance, Ty!" Darren said, not taking his eyes off Cole. "This kid ruined my ride. He has it coming!"

"No, he doesn't," Ty said. He nodded at Cole. "Go on, take off."

Cole started to move past Darren. But Darren shifted in front of him. "What's the matter, karate boy? You chicken or something?"

"N-no," Cole stammered. "I — I'm not supposed to use karate outside of the dojo. It's against the rules."

Darren gave a harsh bark of laughter. "Dude, don't you know that rules are made to be broken?"

Then he rolled up his sleeve and flexed his bicep muscle. "I don't blame you for running away. I doubt any karate move would be a match for *this*!" He slapped the muscle with the flat of his hand. It made a loud *smack*.

"Actually, Darren," Ty said mildly, "if this kid knows enough karate, he could probably take you."

Darren snorted with derision. "Yeah, right!"

Ty ignored him. "What belt are you, kid?"

"Blue," Cole replied.

"Then you know some grappling and takedowns, maybe some locks, right?"

Cole nodded, his eyes wide. He'd started learning the self-defense techniques Ty mentioned back when he was a purple belt. But how did Ty know about them? He was tempted to ask him. But he wanted to get away from Darren even more. Asking questions would only keep him there, so he kept his mouth closed.

Ty turned back to Darren. "He could take you all right. But if you want to embarrass yourself —" he shrugged, "— go ahead and try to hit him."

At those words, a slow smile spread across Darren's face — and every fiber in Cole's body tensed in anticipation of the blow that was about to come.

7

But to Cole's surprise — and great relief — Darren didn't take a swing at him. He turned away.

"Aw, forget it," the teen said. "He's not worth the trouble. Come on, guys, let's get out of here." With that, he put one foot on his skateboard and pushed off with the other. The bucktoothed kid and the one who had spit followed close behind.

Ty was about to join them when Cole stopped him.

"I — I — thanks," he mumbled.

"No problem. What's your name?"

"I'm Cole."

"Well, Cole, if I were you, I'd steer clear of Darren. He may have walked away this time. But if he catches you alone . . ."

He left the rest unspoken, but Cole understood

what he meant. If Darren caught him alone, the older boy wouldn't hesitate to come after him.

Once more, Cole thanked him.

Ty waved it off. "I wasn't kidding, you know," he said. "With your skills, I think you could've taken him if you were ready."

Cole couldn't contain his curiosity any longer. "How do you know about my skills?" he blurted.

Ty looked away. "Simple. I used to take karate."

"You did? Where'd you train? Do you know Sensei Joe? What belt did you reach?" The questions came pouring out.

Ty didn't answer any of them. Instead, he said, "My karate days are ancient history." Then he stepped on his board, pushed off, and slalomed down the bike path after the others. "Remember what I said about Darren," he called as he went.

After Ty left, there was nothing for Cole to do but head home. As he walked, it started to rain. He pulled his hood up over his head with an absentminded tug, too busy thinking about what had just happened to notice that he was getting soaked to the skin.

But his mother noticed. "You look like something the cat dragged in!" she exclaimed when he entered the kitchen twenty minutes later. She sent him up-stairs to take a hot shower before dinner.

He thought about Ty's final warning while under the warm spray. He shifted uneasily. Did Ty really think Darren planned to come after him?

If he does, he thought, *will I be able to defend myself?*

Cole had never used karate on someone who wasn't a fellow student. And even when he practiced it at the dojo, he sometimes messed up — like today, when he forgot how to do the wrist grab and didn't block well while doing kumite number three.

What if Darren attacks me, and I forget everything I've ever learned?

With that dismal thought in his brain, he turned off the water and climbed out of the shower. But as he toweled off, he realized Ty had already given him the solution to that problem.

Steer clear of Darren, he'd said.

Cole wiped a circle in the fog from the bathroom mirror and stared at his reflection.

Well, that's just what I'm going to do! It shouldn't be too difficult. After all, he's gotta be in high school. What're the chances that we'll meet?

He slicked his hair down with a few swipes of his comb. Then he put on a change of clothes and opened the bathroom door. Delicious food smells wafted in, mingling with the last of the steam from his shower.

Sniffing the air appreciatively, Cole hurried downstairs to eat. By the time he reached the kitchen, he was determined to put Darren out of his mind for good.

I have more important things to worry about, he thought as he poured himself a tall glass of cold milk, *like practicing for my green belt test and making up a kata!*

8

You did *what*?" Cole stared at Marty, horrified. It was the next morning and he had just run into his friend in the hallway at school. He was usually happy to see Marty. But right now, he wanted to strangle him.

That's because Marty had just informed him that he had invited Monique to practice karate with them that afternoon.

"How could you do that to me?" Cole fumed. "You know she drives me crazy!"

Marty held up his hands. "Before you freak out completely, just listen to why I asked her to join us!"

Cole blew out a long breath. "This should be good," he muttered, crossing his arms over his chest and fixing Marty with a glare.

"Number one," Marty said, "she became a green belt before we did —"

"As she loves to point out whenever she can!" Cole interrupted.

Marty lifted his eyebrows. "Will you let me finish, please?"

"Okay, okay," Cole growled.

"Since she's already a green belt, she knows what that test will be like. I thought maybe she could give you some pointers."

Cole snorted. "Please tell me that's not the only reason you're forcing her on me!"

"No! She's really good at performing katas, too. I figured with her help our katas for the contest might stand a better chance of winning!"

Cole narrowed his eyes. "What makes you think she won't give us lousy advice? I mean, come on, what's in it for her if she helps us with our katas? Or me with my belt test, for that matter?"

Marty sighed. "Those questions bring me to the third reason I invited her."

"Which is . . . ?"

"It's going to sound lame."

"Just tell me!"

Marty hung his head and shuffled his feet. "I feel sorry for her, all right? Yeah, she can be a royal pain, and yeah, she's a total karate know-it-all." He looked searchingly at Cole. "But I remember how we all used to be friends. Don't you?"

Cole stared at Marty for a long moment. Then he unfolded his arms. "I guess I do. But I still wish you had waited to be her friend again until *after* the kata contest and my test — or at least asked me before you invited her to join us!"

Marty laughed. "Don't worry. It'll be fine. You'll see!"

"Maybe," Cole grumbled.

After school, Cole strapped his duffel bag of karate gear to his bike rack and rode to Marty's house. He wasn't sure if he'd need his stuff, but he figured it was better to have it than not.

After he arrived, he and Marty went downstairs to the basement and pushed the furniture to the walls so they would have enough room to move freely.

Monique showed up ten minutes later. "Hi," she said, shooting Cole a tentative smile as she stowed her own bag of karate equipment next to the sofa. "I hope you don't mind my being here, too."

Marty gave Cole a look. "Be nice!" the look warned.

"The more the merrier," Cole said. He took off his

socks, balled them up, and threw them onto an easy chair. Then he sat on the floor and started to stretch. The others followed his example, and for the next ten minutes the only sound in the basement was their breathing. When their muscles were warm, they were ready to begin.

"So, how about we work on the kata contest stuff first?" Cole suggested.

"Can't we start with something else?" Monique asked reluctantly. "I'm not even sure the contest is such a great idea."

"Huh? Why not?" Marty asked.

Monique raised a shoulder. "Say someone who entered made up a really dumb kata. Don't you think it'd be a waste of time to have to sit and watch it? Or learn it?"

Cole rolled his eyes. "Well, if you don't want to work on the contest stuff, then what *do* you want to do?"

"Marty said you needed help with your test material," Monique ventured. "I'd be happy to critique a few of your katas for you."

"I bet you would," Cole muttered under his breath.

"What did you say?" Monique asked sharply.

Cole glanced at Marty, who gave him the warning look again. "Uh, I said, 'That'd be good!'"

Monique narrowed her eyes as if she didn't believe him. But she didn't say anything. Instead, she perched on the arm of a chair. Marty took a seat next to her. Feeling like he was on display, Cole walked to the middle of the room and faced them.

"Heian One," Monique said primly. "Two moves at a time. I'll call it out. And if I see a mistake," she added, "I'll be sure to stop you."

Cole locked his brown eyes with her blue ones. Then he tightened his lips and forced his eyes front. It was all he could do to keep himself from telling her that he'd rather fail the test than put up with this!

9

Go for it, man!"

Marty's loud, encouraging cheer broke some of the tension in the room. "Give Heian One everything you've got!"

Heian One was the name of the first kata they had learned as karate students. Cole had once read that *heian* was a Japanese term often translated as "peaceful mind." Cole hadn't understood why a sequence of fighting moves would have that name, and had asked Sensei Joe about it one class.

"It's a good question," Sensei Joe had responded. He had gathered the rest of the class around then so they could all hear his answer.

"Katas like Heian One were created long ago. One of their purposes was to train students to fend off multiple opponents. In fact, when you perform a kata next time, imagine that you're surrounded by many attackers. If you do, it may help you give your moves more power. Observe."

He stepped away from them to the middle of the dojo. Then he widened his eyes as if seeing a horde of angry people coming toward him. "Look out! The first guy is coming at you with a punch! What do you do?"

He whipped his palm across his body, a palm-heel block. "You block his blow to protect yourself, that's what you do. And then *you* strike at *him*!"

He shot his fist out straight. "Boom! Now he's down —" he spun around and pointed at an imaginary foe, "— but look out, here comes his buddy up on your left! Quick, block again, then strike!"

Sensei Joe continued to shift around, throwing blocks, landing strikes, and lashing out with kicks against pretend assailants. "Block, strike, turn!" he called. "Block, kick, strike, pivot! Use your legs to put *oomph* into your moves! Make every one count as you take care of each attacker, one after another!"

At last, he stopped. With a smile and swipe at the sweat beading his brow, he said, "Think like that, and you'll be amazed at how much more urgency goes into every single move. Trust me; it works!"

Then he gestured to Cole. "Now can you see why *heian* is often translated as *peaceful mind*?"

Cole scratched his head, thinking. "Because the person who knows how to do those katas knows how to defend himself — and so has peace of mind?" he guessed.

"Exactly!"

Cole thought of that conversation now as he stood waiting to do Heian One in Marty's basement. He made a mental note to think of being attacked when he began.

Monique smoothed a stray red curl from her face and said, "Ready stance."

Cole balled his hands into loose fists and held them out in front of him. His gaze was focused straight ahead, his feet were slightly apart, and his knees were bent.

"Bow," Monique commanded.

Cole slid one foot to the other, flattened his hands against his thighs, and bent from the waist. Then he returned to the ready position.

"Two moves at a time," Monique reminded him. "On my command." She waited a beat and then said, "Step!"

Cole snapped his left fist up to his right ear,

stretched his right arm down in front of him, spun a quarter turn to the left, and shifted his feet into a cat stance — feet side by side, knees bent, left heel raised, and right leg supporting most of his weight. Everything moved at the same time, in one fluid motion.

He paused in this position for a split second. Then he whipped his fist down and across his body — a downward block — while sliding his left foot forward. Now he was in a front stance. His legs were shoulder-width apart, weight forward, and both knees were bent.

Again, Cole paused for a fraction of a beat. Then, moving foot and fist at the same time, he swept his right foot in an arc — in to his left and then out into a front stance — and punched with his right hand. Just before he finished the punch, he twisted his fist over. If his knuckles had actually made contact with a body, the end twist would have stretched the skin and the nerves beneath it uncomfortably tight, adding to the pain of the punch itself.

"Ki-ai!" he shouted.

"Step!" Monique called.

Now Cole brought his right fist up to his left ear. He spun around to the right 180 degrees and stepped forward with another strong downward block.

He started to pull back into a cat stance for the next move, a right straight-in shuto, when Monique barked, "Stop!"

Cole dropped his hands and stared at her. "What? Did I do something wrong?"

"It's not what you *did*, it's what you *forgot* to do," she admonished. "Go back to the straight-in punch."

He turned around and got into position: right front stance, right arm out as if he had just punched.

"Step!"

He repeated the turn-around/downward block. She stopped him once more.

"You forgot again," she said in a singsong voice.

"Forgot *what*?"

"You have to square off with the stretch and cat stance *before* you go into the second downward block." She shook her head. "If you leave out that transition during the test, the senseis will be all over you."

"Big deal!" Cole retorted, "I'm used to that kind of treatment, thanks to you!"

10

Cole regretted the words the moment he said them. Sure, he was mad at Monique for correcting him. But she was right. He *had* left out the transition — and the senseis *would* notice. Maybe it would affect the outcome of the test, maybe it wouldn't. Regardless, he couldn't fix the mistake if he didn't know about it.

But there was another reason he regretted his angry retort. From the look on Monique's face, he knew his words had stung badly.

She slipped out of her chair and grabbed her gear bag. "I was only trying to help," she mumbled. "But maybe I should go."

Cole was about to tell her to stay when Marty beat him to the punch. "Come on, Monique, don't go! We've barely started."

She hesitated but didn't put her bag down.

"I'll give you ice cream later if you stay!" Marty coaxed, his voice laced with laughter.

A smile twitched at the corners of Monique's lips. "What flavor?"

"Your favorite: mint chocolate chip!"

"That's not her favorite," Cole cut in. "Rocky road is."

Monique looked at him with surprise. Then she broke into a wide grin. "I can't believe you remember that!"

Cole shrugged, suddenly embarrassed. "I might forget some things, like a transition in a kata," he said, "but other things I remember."

Marty smiled at them both, took the bag from Monique's hand, and stuck it behind the sofa. Then he planted himself on the sofa, as if to guard the bag.

Cole, meanwhile, returned to the ready position. "I'd like to start Heian One again. And this time, I promise not to get mad when you correct me."

Marty flopped back into his chair. But Monique stayed standing, chewing her lip as if debating whether to say something. Finally, she spoke up. "Can I make a suggestion? It's something Sensei Ann told me to try."

"What?"

"Pretend you're doing the kata underwater."

Cole furrowed his brow in confusion. "Underwater? Why?"

"It'll force you to go re-e-ally slo-o-ow-ly," Monique explained, drawing out the last words to emphasize her point. "Then you can focus on hitting every move. Watch."

She got into ready stance, bowed, and straightened. Then she began to do Heian One in ultra-slow motion. Each of the kata's blocks, punches, and shutos was deliberate. Every stance was precisely positioned.

"You look like that group of people in the park who do tai chi every Sunday afternoon," Marty said, laughing.

"Shhhh!" Monique whispered. "I'm focusing here."

She finally finished, straightened, and smiled with a trace of embarrassment. "I know it looks kind of silly. But it really helped me hone my katas."

Cole and Marty exchanged glances. Then Cole shrugged. "What the heck, I'll give it a try."

Marty hopped up. "I want to do it, too! In fact, I'll bet I can do it slower than you can!"

Monique laughed and settled into her easy chair. "Ooooo-kaaaaay," she intoned. "Re-aaa-dy? Sssss-teeee-p!"

11

Heian One usually took less than a minute to perform. This time, with Marty and Cole vying to out-slow each other, it took closer to ten! Cole was concentrating so hard on every move, he started to sweat. He was amazed to discover that he felt tired when he was done.

"Whew!" he said, collapsing onto the floor. "Those tai chi people get a better workout than I thought!"

"Want to go on to Heian Two?" Monique asked.

Marty shook out his arms and legs. "Give me two minutes," he said. "Then I will."

"Okay, but I'm timing you!" Monique said. She looked up at the clock — and then, with an alarmed cry, jumped out of her chair. "Oh, man, is that the time? I have to leave!"

"But we haven't worked on the katas for the contest

yet," Marty protested. "I was really hoping you'd help me with mine."

Monique shook her head with regret. "Sorry, Marty, but I promised my mom I'd be home to babysit my little sister so she could go to her book club tonight. And I still have to do my homework, too. See you, guys!"

She took the stairs two at a time.

"What about the ice cream?" Marty called after her.

"I'll take a rain check!" came her reply.

A moment later, the front door slammed. When it did, it seemed to Cole as if some of the energy in the room had left with her.

He sat up. "I guess we could do Heian Two in slow motion without her," he said. But his heart wasn't really in it anymore.

Marty didn't look any more enthusiastic. Then he brightened. "I've got a better idea," he said. "Let's go polish off that ice cream!"

One quart of mint chocolate chip ice cream later, the boys returned to the basement.

"All right, time to get down to business," Marty said. "Let's — oh, no!"

"What's wrong?"

Marty reached behind the sofa. "Monique forgot

her stuff." He lifted her duffel bag to show Cole. As he did, a sheet of paper fluttered out of the side pocket.

Cole grabbed the paper just before it hit the floor. It crinkled in his grasp. He laid it on a nearby table and started to smooth it out. He saw then that there was writing on it. A few words — *punch, knee, block* — jumped out at him.

"Marty, come take a look at this," he said.

"What is it?" Marty asked curiously.

"It looks like a kata," Cole replied. "But if it is, it's not one I recognize. Do you?"

Marty bent over the paper, too. "Recognize it? I can barely read it!" he said with a laugh. "That Monique sure has lousy handwriting, doesn't she?"

"Mmmm." Cole squinted, working to decipher the words.

"Think it's part of the green belt curriculum?" Marty asked.

Cole read through the list of moves again. Realization dawned on him. "It's not part of the green belt stuff. Monique made up this kata, I'd bet you anything!"

"What?" Marty wrinkled his nose. "Didn't she say she wasn't going to enter the contest? That watching made-up katas would be a waste of time or something?"

"That's what she *said*," Cole replied, suddenly angry. "But obviously, she wasn't telling us the truth."

"Huh? Why would she lie?"

"I can think of two reasons," Cole said through gritted teeth. "One, she didn't want to have to share her precious kata with us. And two, she wanted us to think the contest was lame so we wouldn't enter it!"

"Why wouldn't she want us to enter?"

Cole ran his fingers through his hair in exasperation. "Isn't it obvious? The fewer the contestants, the better chance she'll have of winning! It's the same old story — she'll do *anything* to stay one step ahead of us!"

12

Marty backed away from the table, holding up his hands in protest. "Whoa, whoa, whoa, Cole," he said. "You don't really believe that, do you?"

Cole crossed his arms over his chest and gave a curt nod.

"There could be all kinds of other reasons why she didn't tell us about her kata," Marty continued.

"Oh, yeah? Name one!"

"Well . . . maybe she forgot about it. Or, um, maybe it's not even hers! Or . . ." Marty's voice trailed off with a sigh. "Okay, I don't know why she kept it a secret."

He came back to the table. "Is it any good?"

Cole scanned the list of moves again. "I can't tell just by reading it," he said. "I'd have to do it." He pushed the paper closer to Marty. "Here. Call out the moves for me."

Marty hesitated. Then he nodded.

Cole walked to the center of the room and got into ready position. "All right, what's first?"

Marty consulted the sheet. "Bow."

Cole rolled his eyes. "Duh! That's how every kata starts!" But he bowed all the same. "Now what?"

"The first move is a right upward block, but stepping back with the left foot instead of stepping forward with the right."

"Got it." Cole formed a plus sign with his forearms. The left was closer to his chest and pointed up; the right was parallel to the floor and outside the left. Both hands were fisted and faced inward.

Then he took one step backward with his left foot. As he did, he moved his left arm as if someone were yanking back on his elbow. His right arm, meanwhile, swept up past his face. At the last second, he flipped the arm with an outward thrust as if to repel a blow aimed at his skull.

He froze in that position, waiting for Marty to tell him what to do next.

"Left palm-heel strike," Marty said.

Like a well-oiled machine with multiple working parts, Cole lowered his right arm so his fist was at his hip, circled his left foot in to the right and out into a left front stance, and drove the heel of his left hand forward.

"*Wham,*" he whispered, pretending to hit a target at jaw-height.

"Good. Now turn to the right into a cat stance, pull both hands to your right side, and do a right low punch," Marty instructed.

Cole hesitated. "A full turn to the back, or just a quarter turn? And what position are my hands in?"

Marty looked at the sheet. "Quarter turn," he amended. "Sorry. And hands are fisted, left above right."

"Left fist down, right up. No problem." Cole drew his hands across his body and spun forty-five degrees to the right, coming to a stop in a cat stance. His left leg supported most of his weight. His right was bent, heel raised and near his left toes. Then, using his elbow as a pivot point, he swept his right forearm up and out across his body, like a clock hand moving from six to twelve.

From there, he stepped forward with a right punch aimed just below belt level.

"Left downward block," Marty instructed. "Then a right front snap kick."

Cole moved his right arm over as if to protect his lower body and swept his left hand up to his right ear. Then he stepped into a left front stance and swept his left arm down across his body. Then he kicked with his right leg, ending the move in a right front stance.

He waited for the next command. When it didn't come, he turned to look at Marty. Marty was gnawing on a fingernail.

"What's wrong?" Cole asked.

Marty lowered his hand. "I feel weird doing Monique's kata without her permission," he admitted.

Cole stalked over to the table and pulled the paper out of Marty's grasp. "Look at it this way," he said. "If she enters the contest and wins, then we'll be that much further ahead in learning her kata. And if she doesn't enter" — he shrugged — "well, maybe one of us can use her kata instead."

Marty's jaw dropped. "You did *not* just say that. Tell me you did not just suggest that we steal our friend's work!"

"Friend? Ha!" Cole snorted like an angry bull and shook the paper in Marty's face. "If she was really our friend, then she would have shared this with us instead of hiding it from us. But I'm going to teach her a lesson. I'm going to learn this if it's the last thing I do!"

Marty snatched the paper out of Cole's hand. "No, you're not," he said in a low voice. "I won't let you."

13

Cole stared at Marty. But Marty held his ground.

"I won't let you," he repeated. "It's not" — he stopped as if searching for the right thing to say — "it's not the karate way."

Cole looked away, deflated. "Okay," he mumbled. "I don't know what I was thinking."

Marty visibly relaxed. "Good thing you came to your senses," he said as he returned the paper to Monique's bag. "Otherwise, I would have had to bring down my world-famous 'rain of pain' on your head."

Cole snorted. "'Rain of pain?' It can't be that famous, because I don't know about it!"

"You don't know about it because you go unconscious whenever I deliver it!" Marty said. "Like now!"

He suddenly wheeled around and leaped on top of Cole, pummeling him with rapid but light punches as they collapsed to the floor. "Do you not fear the 'rain of pain' now?" Marty said, deepening his voice.

Cole would have answered, but he was laughing too hard to even draw breath. "Stop," he finally managed to gasp, "I fear! I fear!"

Marty hopped to his feet, grinned, and pointed a finger at Cole. "Let that be a lesson to you, peon," he intoned ominously. "Now come on," he added in his normal voice. "Let's start making up our *own* katas, okay?"

Cole looked at the clock. "I have to leave in a little while," he said. "So would you mind if we worked on my grappling for the test instead?"

Grappling was another form of self-defense. The point of the moves was to first free oneself from an attacker and then to get control of the assailant by using a joint lock, a throw, or a takedown.

"We can always do katas on our own," Cole added, "but I need a body for grappling."

Marty bowed low. "Then allow me to be that body! Do you want to do the moves in order, or do you want me to attack you at random?"

"Random would be better, I think."

Marty nodded. Without warning, he grabbed Cole's right wrist and threw a hook punch at his head.

Cole reacted instinctively by using grappling move number one.

Thump! He stopped the punch with a left outward block. *Zip!* He delivered a shuto to Marty's neck with that same hand. Then he brought his captured hand up, wrapped his free hand around Marty's hand, and dug his fingertips into the base of Marty's thumb. That move loosened Marty's grasp just enough for him roll his own hand out. Now, with one hand pressed against Marty's knuckles and the other digging into his thumb, he wrenched Marty's wrist into an awkward — and potentially painful — angle.

Right as Cole started to twist, Marty slapped his thigh. That slap was the signal used by karate students to tell their partner that they had started to feel pain. When Cole heard it, he let go instantly. Marty rubbed his wrist and nodded.

"You got that one down cold!" he said. "Ready for the next?"

Marty spent the next twenty minutes attacking Cole. Sometimes he grabbed him with two hands by the shirt front. Other times he took hold of his wrist and threw a punch. And a few times, he circled behind Cole and caught him in a bear hug.

Cole fended off each attack as best he could. He accidentally hit Marty too hard with one move, but Marty didn't mind. He knew such mistakes could happen, because he had made them himself.

By the end, both boys were breathing hard. "I gotta go soon," Cole said, glancing at the clock.

"Let me give you something to drink before you go," Marty said. "You're sweating like a pig!"

As they climbed the stairs, the phone rang. Marty picked up his pace to answer it.

"Hey, Mrs. Richards," Marty said. "He's right here."

"Hi, Mom," Cole said after he took the phone from Marty. "I'm leaving in five minutes, so I should be home in less than half an hour. Okay? Bye!"

He hung up, finished the lemonade Marty had given him in one gulp, and hurried to the basement to collect his things. He stuffed his feet into his socks, put on his coat, and gear in hand, started back for the stairs. Then he paused.

Monique's bag was still on the sofa. A corner of the paper with the handwritten kata was sticking out of the pocket.

I bet that's her only copy, he thought. *If she didn't have it, she'd be back to square one. She might even drop out of the contest altogether. And if I enter —*

"Hey, did you get lost or something?" Marty called from the top of the stairs.

Cole jumped. "No, no, just — putting on my jacket!" he answered. With a swift, furtive movement, he plucked the kata from Monique's bag and shoved it in his pocket. "Here I come!" he cried.

Outside in the driveway, Cole busied himself with strapping his gear bag to his bike rack. Then he put on his helmet and adjusted the straps.

"All right, you're good to go!" Marty said, slapping him on the back. "And Cole? About Monique's kata?"

Cole froze. "Yeah?"

"Thanks for not stealing it."

14

Cole ducked his head so Marty couldn't see the deep flush that had infused his face.

"Yeah, okay," he mumbled. "See you later."

"Not if I see you first!"

Cole wheeled his bicycle through Marty's backyard to the bike path entrance. With every step, he could hear the paper in his pocket crinkle. It sounded like fire — and felt like it, too, as if it was burning a hole right through the fabric.

I should go put it back, he thought.

But he didn't. Instead, he swung his leg over the bike's bar, put his foot on a pedal, and took off. As he rode, the hum of the tires on the pavement and the wind whipping past his ears drowned out the sound of crinkling paper. He almost forgot the sheet was even in his pocket.

Almost.

He had been riding for ten minutes when suddenly, he heard a loud *pop*. A few minutes later, he noticed that the rim of his front tire was a lot closer to the ground.

Oh, great, he groaned to himself. *A flat!*

He braked to a stop and got off the bike. Sure enough, the tire was completely out of air.

He put down the kickstand and stood back to consider his options. He could turn around, walk the bike back to Marty's house, and ask Mrs. Bronson to give him a ride. Or, he could walk the bike to his own house. He shifted his feet. The paper in his pocket rustled.

That decided it. He would continue to his house. He nudged the kickstand back up and grabbed hold of the handlebars.

As he pushed the bike along, the late afternoon light began to fade. Creatures that grew active at twilight emerged — creatures like an annoying swarm of flies that danced just in front of his face and others that were more pleasant, like the tiny spring peeper frogs that chirped unseen in the nearby wetlands.

He plodded on, batting flies and wishing his bike had

a tire repair kit. Then he rounded a bend in the path and realized with a start that he wasn't far from the karate dojo.

If someone's there, maybe I can stop in and call Mom, he thought.

He walked a little faster. His heart leaped when he saw light coming from the dojo office window. He parked his bike on the edge of the path and hurried to the door.

Snap! Just as he was about to knock, he heard a sound like a tree branch breaking behind him. He looked over his shoulder.

There was nothing there.

He shrugged and turned back. At that same moment, the main room of the dojo suddenly blazed with light. A window popped open and voices filtered out.

Angry voices. He thought he recognized Sensei Ann. Then he frowned. He recognized the other as well. *Monique! What is she doing here?* he thought. *She said she was going home to babysit her sister! And why was she arguing with Sensei Ann?*

Feeling like a thief, he moved to the window to peek inside. What he saw made him gasp with alarm.

Sensei Ann was holding a knife to Monique's throat!

15

Cole's heart hammered in his chest, threatening to burst with every beat. Then he blinked, looked again, and heaved a huge sigh of relief.

The knife wasn't real. It was one of the dojo's practice blades, made of black foam and rubber and shaped to resemble a knife. Sensei Ann was working with Monique on techniques to defend against weapons.

His heartbeat slowly returned to normal.

Then it sped up again — not with fear, however, but with sudden anger.

Monique is getting a private lesson, not babysitting. Another lie!

Movement inside the dojo caught his eye again. Curiosity battled with his anger. He himself had only just begun to learn knife defense. Part of him wanted to burst into the dojo and confront Monique with her lie. Another part wanted to eavesdrop on her lesson and pick up a few pointers.

In the end, curiosity won out. He edged closer to the window to get a better view.

Suddenly, there was a loud crash behind him. He whirled around and saw his bike lying on its side. Its back wheel spun slowly, the shiny spokes winking in the fading twilight.

"What the heck was that?" Sensei Ann said.

Cole heard light footsteps crossing the dojo floor toward his window. He ducked down and flattened himself against the dojo's wall.

"Do you see anything?" he heard Monique say from directly above his head.

He held his breath. Could they see his bike in the shadows — and if they did, would they realize someone was just outside?

"Must have been an animal in the underbrush," Sensei Ann said after a moment. "It's amazing how much noise one little squirrel can make."

"Are you sure that's all it was?" Monique didn't

sound convinced. "I could have sworn I saw something bigger than a squirrel moving around out there."

"Well, whatever it was, it's out there, not in here," Sensei Ann said. "Ready to continue?"

Cole missed Monique's reply, however, because Sensei Ann closed the window. He sat against the wall for a few minutes longer. Then, moving in a crouch, he tiptoed quickly and quietly to his bike, lifted it upright, and started to push it away. He kept to the furthest edge of the path, where he hoped the growing shadows would hide him until he was clear of the dojo completely. Only after he had entered a tree-lined section of the path did he venture back to the middle.

That was close! he thought. *I wonder why my bike fell over? I'm sure I put the kickstand down.*

Snap!

Cole paused. There was that sound again, like a branch being broken underfoot. He looked around. But it was hard to see anything because the branches above shrouded everything in deep shadows.

Probably a squirrel. Or maybe another wild animal.

He noticed then that his gear bag was dangling off his bike rack. If he didn't fix it, it would fall off completely. With an impatient growl, he put the kickstand down and moved to secure it. As he did, he glanced into the gloom.

He didn't want to admit it, but the thought of being alone on the bike path in the dark frightened him — just a little. After all, who knew what —

"Yee-ahhh!"

An unearthly yowl shattered the night air. With a thunderous crash, something came hurtling out of the underbrush. Before Cole could turn to see what it was, strong arms wrapped around his upper body!

"I've got you now!" a guttural voice growled.

Darren!

The name flashed through Cole's brain even as he reacted with pure instinct and adrenaline-charged strength.

Wham! He drove a sharp elbow backward into Darren's ribs. *Thud!* He followed that strike with a downward hammer fist to his attacker's groin area.

"Ooof!" The blows forced Darren to loosen his hold just for a second.

That was all Cole needed. He grabbed hold of Darren's fingers and spun under the teenager's arm. That move flipped Darren's palm upward — and gave Cole, who still had a tight hold on his fingers, control. All he had to do was bend those fingers back from the palm to send pain shooting through Darren's arm.

But suddenly, he heard a familiar sound.

Slap! Slap!

Darren was slapping his thigh, the signal to end a karate maneuver!

16

Stunned, Cole immediately let go of the fingers. "How do you know about the thigh slap?" he demanded.

His assailant straightened — and that's when Cole saw that it wasn't Darren at all.

"*Ty?*" he gasped. "What — what're you doing? Why did you —?"

Ty held up a hand. "Hang on." Then he called, "Okay, fellows, come on out."

One by one, the bucktoothed boy, the one who spit, and finally Darren emerged from the underbrush.

Cole tensed, his eyes shifting from Ty to the three other boys. "What's going on?" he asked.

"I'm really sorry that I scared you like that, Cole," Ty said. "I did it for a good reason."

Cole backed up, still on his guard. "Oh, yeah? What?"

"I had to prove to Darren that if he came after you, you'd wallop him."

Cole blinked. "Huh?"

Ty nodded. "That's right. Darren here was thinking he owed you a payback for ruining his ride yesterday. I convinced him to see you in action before he tried." He glanced over to the other boy. "What do you think of your chances now, Darren?"

Darren gave a low rumble of laughter. "Well, I don't know if he could *wallop* me, not in a face-to-face fist-fight or a wrestling match, anyway. But I think he might be able to stop me!" He aimed a finger gun at Cole then. "Pretty cool moves. You're okay with me, kid. See you around town."

He gestured to the other teenagers that they were leaving. "You coming, Ty?"

"Nah, I'm going to walk Cole home," Ty replied. "But I'll catch up with you guys at school tomorrow. We've got that earthworm dissection in biology first period, right?"

"Eeewww, gross, why'd you remind me?" The buck-toothed teen suddenly looked green. "I hate looking at guts."

"It's just a worm!" the other boy chided. "How much guts can it have?"

"I don't know, but enough to turn me into a vegetarian, I'll bet!"

The three teenagers headed away down the path, laughing — and to his amazement, Cole found he was laughing with them.

Maybe these guys aren't so bad after all, he thought. *Just because they look tough and act tough, doesn't mean they* are *tough.*

"Come on, Cole, let's get you home," Ty said when the others had disappeared. He helped Cole strap his gear bag tightly onto the rack. Then they started down the path.

They were mostly silent as they walked. Then, as they neared the turnoff for Cole's house, Cole abruptly stopped. "Ty, can I ask you something?"

"I guess so," Ty said, but he sounded wary.

"Why did you stop taking karate?"

Ty let out a long breath. "You really want to know?"

Cole nodded.

"Okay, I'll tell you, but first" — he gestured toward the house — "you better go tell your mom that you're home."

Cole looked where Ty was pointing and saw that his mother was standing in the back door, arms folded tightly against her chest. From her posture, Cole could tell she was worried.

"Hey, Mom!" He hurried to her side, explained about the flat, and introduced her to Ty.

"If it's okay with you, Mrs. Richards," Ty said, "I'll help Cole fix his flat and then be on my way."

Mrs. Richards raised her eyebrows but nodded. "That would be very kind of you, Ty. Thank you. I'll open the garage door so you can get in. The tools are all there."

Two minutes later, the flat tire was off the bike and resting on the floor between the boys. But they weren't working on replacing it.

Instead, Ty was telling Cole about when he took karate — and why he had stopped training four years ago.

68

17

I trained at the same place you do, with Sensei Joe," the teenager said. "I started when I was seven years old. By the time I was eleven, I was a green belt."

"Hey, what do you know?" Cole said. "I'm eleven and I'm testing for my green on Sunday."

Ty smiled. "Are you nervous?"

"Nah!" Then Cole grinned sheepishly. "Well, kinda. Okay. Yeah, I'm nervous."

"I remember what that's like," Ty sympathized. "But if you perform all your moves the way you did against my attack tonight, you shouldn't have a problem.

"Anyway," he continued, "I was a green belt. One day after karate class I accidentally left my bo staff back at the dojo." He glanced at Cole. "You have one of those, right?"

Cole nodded. The bo staff was a lightweight

wooden pole that was just slightly taller than he was. His was black with silvery dragons painted on it, but they came in different colors, too. Some of the girls even had pink ones, which he thought was funny; after all, the bo was a weapon, not a plaything!

Ty leaned against the garage wall and stared at the ceiling. "When I realized I didn't have my bo with me, I went back to get it. I was walking by the playground that's near the library — you know the one?"

"Yeah, I used to play there when I was little," Cole said. "It was always crowded with kids."

"Well, that day there were only two people there, a mom and her little girl. The mom was talking on her cell phone. I guess she wasn't getting good reception because she wandered away from the playground. But she left her purse sitting on a bench. As I was passing, I saw a man sneaking up to the bench."

Cole's eyes widened. "He was going to steal the purse?"

"That's what it looked like to me."

"Did you yell to the lady?"

Ty shook his head. "It wouldn't have helped. The guy was so close that even if I warned her, he could have snatched her stuff and run before she had a chance to do anything."

"So what *did* you do?"

Ty closed his eyes as if watching a replay of the scene in his mind. "I started toward the guy. But the little girl must have seen what he was doing, too. She ran to the bench and grabbed the purse before he could. But she fell when she tried to run with it."

Cole held his breath. "What happened then?"

"I got there. I put myself between the thief and the little girl."

"And?"

"And he took a swing at me — a classic, from-behind, full wind-up, hook punch."

"Oh my gosh!" Cole breathed. Then he broke into a smile. "Let me guess: you stopped him with one of the kumites!"

Ty opened his eyes and scrubbed his hands across his face. "No. I didn't do anything! Everything I'd ever learned in karate just seemed to vanish from my brain. I just stood there like a statue and let the guy hit me!"

Cole stared in shock. "You — what?"

"Yeah. Then he yanked the purse right out of the little girl's hands and took off."

Ty drew his legs in to his chest, rested his elbows on his knees, and bent his head down. "I quit karate the next day. I couldn't go back, not after I saw the look on the girl's face. Not after what she said."

"What did she say?"

He lifted his head. "'Why didn't you use karate to stop him?'"

"How did she know you did karate?"

"I was still wearing my gi, remember? But there was something about the way she said it, made me think she knew more about karate than just what the uniform looked like."

"What was her name?"

Ty groaned. "I don't know. I was so ashamed I just ran away. But I'll never forget her. She had these big blue eyes and this head of curly red hair — and she was looking up at me with this completely stunned expression."

Cole sat up straight. "Did you say she had blue eyes and red hair?"

Ty nodded.

Cole's mind was whirring. "You said this happened

four years ago. And you think the girl knew what karate was?"

Ty nodded again. "She seemed to, yeah. Why?"

Cole reached his hand into his pocket and touched the paper with Monique's kata. "No reason."

18

Cole and Ty replaced the flat tire in silence. Cole was too busy pondering a suspicion he had to make conversation. And Ty seemed spent from having told his story. It was only when Ty was ready to leave that Cole roused himself from his reverie.

"Ty, do you miss karate?"

Ty looked surprised at the question. Then he shrugged. "Sure. Sometimes. I never really got into any other sports. Except skateboarding, that is."

"Well, why don't you start taking it again?"

"I don't know, Cole. It's been so long. I bet I don't remember anything. I'd probably have to start all over!"

"You remembered the thigh slap," Cole pointed out.

The older boy laughed. "That was purely instinctive!" he said. "You had a vicious finger lock on me! I may not remember how to do that move, but I sure as

74

heck remember what it felt like to be on the receiving end of it!"

"You should think about coming back," Cole insisted. "I mean, give yourself a break. You were only eleven years old! Who knows what that purse-snatcher might have done to you if you had tried to stop him!"

Ty busied himself with putting the repair tools away. "You know, when the police caught him, they found out he'd been using the stolen money to buy drugs."

Cole flung his arms open. "See? It's probably a good thing you *didn't* do anything! He might have had a knife or a gun or . . ." He broke off, shuddering as he thought of all the terrible possibilities.

"Anyway," he finished, "I bet that little girl didn't really blame you. She was probably too scared to think of anything!"

Ty raised a shoulder. "Since I don't know who she was, I'll never know, will I?" With that, he pushed the toolbox back onto its shelf, waved good-bye, and left.

Cole stood in the garage for a moment longer. "I think I know who she was," he said to no one. "And if I'm right, it explains a whole lot." He clicked off the lights, pushed the button to close the garage door, and went inside.

"Hey, honey," his mother said. "Hang up your coat and come have dinner."

"Okay." But before he put his jacket on the hook, he pulled out Monique's kata. The paper was wrinkled and torn from having been in his pocket. He bit his lip, sorrier than ever that he'd taken it from her bag. But he had, and there was nothing he could do to change that.

He couldn't change it, but he could try to make up for it. He folded the paper a few times and stuck it into his back pocket.

"Hey, Mom," he said when he came into the kitchen, "would it be okay if I used the computer tonight?"

"Going to type up your kata?" she inquired.

"It's something for the contest, yeah," he answered truthfully.

But it wasn't his own kata he typed up later, it was Monique's. When he was done, he saved the document, and then printed it out.

"I'll be in my room!" he yelled to his mother as he carried the printout upstairs. He studied the sheet for a few minutes, then laid it on his bed, stepped back, and followed the moves one by one.

"Ready stance, bow," he murmured. "Step back with left foot, upward block right.

"Step forward left front stance into left palm heel. Do a one-quarter turn to right into cat stance with hands fisted left over right, then into a low right punch. Step forward left front stance with left downward block. Step forward right with right front snap kick."

That's as far as he had gotten in Marty's basement. He double-checked the paper to see what came next.

"Transition one-half turn to the left into left-cross shuto with back stance. Then reach and grab into a right knee followed by a step right into double punch."

To a non-karate student, such instructions might have sounded like complete gibberish. To Cole, they made perfect sense.

He spun out of the right punch and did the left-cross shuto, striking out with the blade of his left hand while dropping down into a back stance and pulling his right hand to a spot at belt height. Next, he twisted to a front stance, raised his hands as if to grab an opponent by the shoulders, and then pulled down while jerking his right knee up.

If he had really been facing an attacker, his knee would have driven into the assailant's stomach. And if that knee hadn't stopped his opponent in his tracks, the two-fisted double punch that came next certainly would have!

Cole stopped then and started from the beginning. Only after he was sure he had the first series of moves down pat did he add on.

Double arm circular throw to the back. Right punch. Left front snap kick. Spin into a right-cross shuto. Another grab and knee. Another double punch. On and on he went, memorizing each move, stopping and beginning again, until at last he reached the final bow that ended Monique's kata.

He flopped onto his bed then, tired but happy.

It was a good kata. That's what he would tell her tomorrow before their karate class — right after he gave her the typed-up copy and confessed to having taken her handwritten version. With any luck, he'd have time to apologize before she could get too furious with him. He might even get the chance to ask her about a certain incident that had happened four years ago at a playground.

But he wasn't sure luck was going to be on his side.

19

As it turned out, Cole didn't even have time to give Monique the typed-up copy of her kata, let alone apologize or ask questions before class. That's because his gi was still in the dryer when he needed to get changed. Therefore, he was five minutes late to class that afternoon.

The students were already working their way through basics when he hurried into the dojo. Sensei Joe instructed him to bow, put on his belt, and join the others.

Cole quickly did so, taking a spot near Marty. "Guess what I did last night?" he whispered to his friend.

Marty turned — Cole stepped back in shock.

Marty looked enraged! "I *know* what you did last night!" he hissed. "When did you turn into such a *jerk*?"

A few other students looked their way. Monique

79

didn't, but Cole could see from the dull red flush creeping up her neck that she had heard them.

He realized then that somehow, Marty knew he had taken the kata. Monique knew, too.

He wanted to explain, to apologize, right then and there, but he couldn't. So instead, he threw himself into doing the basic moves with as much power as he could.

"Ki-ai!" he shouted with every punch, kick, and block.

After ten minutes, Sensei Joe divided the students into two groups. "Purple belts, go with Sensei Duane," he said, pointing to a young man in a black gi. "Blue and green belts, you're with Sensei Dale."

Dale and Duane were brothers and looked so much alike that Cole sometimes got them confused — until they started teaching, that is. Then their different styles set them apart immediately. Dale liked to work on sparring, while Duane preferred to pick apart kata performances.

Cole, Marty, Monique, and two other students hurried to put on their sparring equipment — padded helmets, gloves, and foot protectors — and returned to the section of the dojo covered with floor mats.

Cole tried to get near enough to Marty to whisper his explanation. But Marty just moved away and started talking with the other kids. Then the sparring began and Cole didn't have time for anything but concentrating on the mock-fight.

"Cole," Sensei Dale said, "since you'll be testing for your green belt on Sunday, I want you to partner with someone higher in rank who will really put you through your paces. Monique, would you go with him, please?"

Monique nodded. Then she turned to Cole. A slow, humorless smile crossed her lips. "I'd like nothing better than to take a few swings at him," she murmured.

Cole gulped. Any doubt he had that Monique knew he'd taken her kata vanished with that sentence. She knew. And she was planning to make him pay.

Some of the girl students — and many of the boys, too — were leery when it came to sparring. After all, the purpose of the exercise was to try to land blows on one's opponent while preventing the opponent from doing the same. Although the matches were carefully monitored by the sensei in charge, sometimes those hits, and many of the blocks, too, were harder than expected!

Monique wasn't afraid of getting hit — or of hitting, for that matter. She had lightning-quick reflexes that helped her block incoming strikes before they could reach her. And when she went on the attack, well, Marty's "world-famous rain of pain" was nothing compared to what she could do!

"Oh boy," he heard Marty whisper to the other students, both green belts. "This is going to be interesting."

20

Sensei Dale ordered Marty and the two green belts to each take a corner of the floor.

"You'll be judging the fight," he told them. "When I call stop, it means one of them has made a hit. If you think it was Monique, raise your right hand. If it was Cole, raise your left. A show of one finger means one point for a punch; two means two points for a kick. If you cross your palms in front of your face, it means your vision was blocked and you didn't see who hit who. And if you make a circular motion with your hand, it means one of them made an illegal hit — that'd be one to the face, below the belt, or to the back. Okay?"

The judges nodded. They'd all done this before.

Now Sensei Dale told Monique and Cole to bow to one another and shake hands. Then he stepped back.

Cole stepped back, too. The mat beneath his feet felt soft and squishy. He bounced on his toes, wishing the blows that were about to come would feel soft and squishy, too.

"Ready?" called Sensei Dale.

Cole raised his gloved hands in front of his face. Monique did the same.

"Fight!" their instructor said.

The word was barely out of his mouth when Monique charged, fists flying. Cole turned sideways to give her less of a target and tried to block the punches. He knocked a few away but she landed one to his rib cage. It wasn't a hard blow, but he felt it nonetheless.

"Stop!" Sensei Dale ordered. "Judges?"

All three lifted their right hand with one finger raised.

"One point for Monique," Sensei Dale agreed. "Ready? Fight!"

This time, Cole didn't wait for her to come to him. He shuffled forward and, with a quick whipping motion, kicked at her with a roundhouse intended for her hip.

But before his foot could touch, she raised her leg, knee bent, and blocked him. Then she drove in with a one-two delivery to his middle!

"Stop!" Three right fingers sailed into the air. "Monique again. Two to zero."

Cole lifted his hands, waiting for the signal to fight. Instead, Sensei Dale said, "Cole, remember to keep your hands up at all times. You dropped them when you kicked. That's how she got those punches in so easily. Right?"

Cole flushed at his mistake and then nodded that he understood. *It won't happen again,* he told himself.

It didn't, but other mistakes did.

The next time he kicked, he threw his whole body behind it — only to feel his standing foot slip out from under him! He landed with a thud on the mat and Monique hadn't even laid a finger on him.

Then, he neglected to watch her legs as well as her fists. So when she leveled a kick at him, her foot thwacked his side for two points.

Finally, he forgot a simple but important rule, one that had been drilled into him early on in his training: never turn your back on your opponent. He spun away from her at one point, only to turn back into her oncoming fist.

When the match finally ended, he had earned just one point. She had earned five, a sound victory. With a triumphant smile, she pulled off her helmet, shook out her hair, and went to the cubbies to put her gear away.

Now! Cole's mind screamed at him as he followed her to do the same. *Apologize now!*

But he was too late. She had moved into one of the judge's spots. After a moment, he moved to another. Once more, he tried to catch Marty's eye. But Marty refused to look at him — not then, while he was still judging, or after he had his turn in the sparring ring, or later, when they were performing katas with Sensei Duane.

Class ended soon afterward. The senseis bowed them out and one by one the students retrieved their belongings. Cole didn't grab his bag, however. Instead, he pulled out the typed-up kata and left everything else behind. Then he worked his way through the crush of students, looking for Monique.

He found Marty instead.

Or rather, Marty found him. He grabbed Cole by the arm, pulled him into a side storage room and, hands on hips, demanded, "Well?"

21

Okay, okay, I took it!" Cole confessed. Then he waved the paper in his hand in front of Marty's face. "But look, I brought it back, typed and everything!"

Marty grabbed the sheet from his hand and turned to leave.

"Wait!" Cole cried. To his relief, Marty hesitated.

"It was a terrible, rotten, stupid, mean thing that I did, stealing Monique's kata," he admitted, his words coming out in a rush.

"You left out awful, nasty, cruel, and downright horrible," Marty muttered. "What were you thinking, man?"

"I wasn't thinking. I was angry at her for hiding it from us." He frowned suddenly. "That wasn't the only thing she was hiding, you know. She didn't have to leave to babysit her sister last night. She left to —"

"Come here and have a karate lesson with Sensei

Ann," Marty finished. "I know. She told me when she called to see if her bag was at my house."

"She . . . did?"

"Yeah. She said she had mixed up the days. Last night was her private lesson. Tonight is when she babysits for her sister."

"Oh." Any righteous anger Cole might have believed he deserved to feel vanished instantly. In its place rose a wave of shame. He slumped against the wall. "Marty, I feel so badly about taking that kata," he said, his voice low. "Do you think you can forgive me?"

Marty let out a long breath. "Yeah, I'll forgive you. I know you were mad. But that didn't give you the right to steal. And if you ever do anything like that again —"

"I won't!" Cole promised. He glanced out toward the main dojo. Most of the students, including Monique, he saw, had packed up and left, making way for a group of adults to train. He sighed with frustration.

"I guess I can't apologize to Monique now," he said.

Marty laid a hand on his shoulder. "Dude, you're going to have to do a lot more than just apologize. I've never seen her so angry, or hurt, either."

Cole rubbed his shoulder where one of her punches had landed earlier. "Yeah, I kind of figured that out during sparring," he said ruefully. "You think she got it out of her system?"

Marty shook his head.

"I didn't think so," Cole said. "I guess I'll have to think of something else."

As he spoke, he caught sight of the paper in Marty's hand. He pushed himself off the wall, thinking hard. Then he smiled. "Marty, I might have a way of showing her how sorry I am," he said. "But I'm going to need your help!"

With that, he took the kata from his friend and began to explain his plan. Marty nodded as he listened. When Cole was done, he had two questions.

"Will it be just you and me, or the whole class?" he asked.

"Just us. If too many people know, they might accidentally ruin the surprise."

"Good point. Second question." Marty fixed Cole with a meaningful stare. "Are you going to confess to Monique beforehand?"

Cole deliberated before answering. "If I get the

chance, I will. But if I don't, then I *promise* I'll do it after. Okay?"

Marty nodded. "Then I'll help you. In fact, if my mom will let me, we can start tonight over at your house."

The two boys left the storage room. Marty got permission from his mother to go to Cole's house instead of his own. They gathered up their belongings and hurried to the door.

But as they were walking through the waiting area beyond the main dojo, Cole suddenly stopped. The walls of the waiting area were decorated with old photographs of former karate classes. One of the photos had caught Cole's eye. It was of a green belt class. In the center of the shot was a much younger Ty!

"What're you looking at?" Marty asked curiously.

Cole tapped the glass covering the photo. "See that kid?"

Marty squinted. "Yeah?"

"I met him the other day."

Marty shrugged. "So?"

"So," Cole said, "I'm pretty sure he's the reason

Monique is a green belt now. But he doesn't know that — and neither does she!"

He laughed at the look of complete confusion on Marty's face. "Come on, let's go," he said as they stepped outside the dojo together. "I'll tell you all about it on the way to my house!"

22

"Let me get this straight," Marty said as they walked through Cole's backyard twenty minutes later. "Ty used to take karate at our dojo. He was a green belt when you and Monique first started. He saw a guy about to steal Monique's mom's purse. He tried to stop him but got belted in the shoulder for his trouble. Monique was there and saw everything —"

"She tried to save the purse, too, remember," Cole interrupted.

"Right. The guy yanked it right out of her hands."

Marty headed down the stairs to Cole's basement with Cole right behind him. "So Ty starts out looking like some kind of superhero, stepping in to save the day. But he ends up looking — and worse, *feeling* — like a loser because he didn't use karate. And that's why he decided to quit?"

Cole nodded.

"But how does his quitting make Monique a green belt?" Marty wanted to know.

"It wasn't his quitting," Cole corrected. He sat down to remove his socks. "Here's what I think: When she saw Ty freeze and when the thief snatched the purse from her, she decided right then and there to learn as much karate as she could. That way, if she was ever in that kind of situation again, she wouldn't have to depend on someone else to help her."

Marty looked thoughtful. "I bet she was scared, too. That might have made her want to take extra lessons."

"You could be right," Cole agreed. "The more karate she learned, the more confidence she'd have another time."

The boys were silent for a moment. Then Marty looked at him sideways and asked, "Do you think you'd be able to use your karate if you got into that situation?"

Cole thought about how he'd reacted when Ty had surprised him on the bike path. "You know what? I think I would. But I sure hope I never have to find out."

He stood up then. "Well, you ready to get to work?"

Marty stood up, too. "I sure am."

"Then let's go — we've got a kata contest to win!"

Cole and Marty worked together for an hour before Mrs. Bronson came to get her son. There was no karate class the next afternoon, so they met at Cole's house then, too. Marty looked dazed when he arrived.

"Monique cornered me after school," he groaned as he helped Cole push the furniture to the sides of the basement. "I had to come up with an excuse why I couldn't go over her kata contest entry with her! Now she's mad at both of us."

Cole had purposefully avoided Monique since their last karate class. It hadn't been difficult, since she had been steering clear of him, too. Cole had been hoping to run into Ty, but so far, he hadn't seen the teenager. He didn't know his last name, either, so he had no way of contacting him by phone.

So in the end, he did the only thing he could think of doing. During his free period of school on Friday, he wrote Ty a letter inviting him to the kata contest on Sunday. After school, he put the letter in an envelope with *Ty* written on it, put the envelope in a plastic baggie, and taped the whole thing to the brick wall where they'd first met.

Then he hurried home to meet Marty for another practice session. He had hoped that Marty would be able to sleep at his house, so they could begin practicing again early Saturday morning. But Mrs. Bronson shook her head when Marty asked.

"We have your cousin April's birthday party to go to," she reminded him.

"Can't I stay here instead?" Marty begged. "April's only a year old! She won't even know I'm missing!"

"*I'll* know you're missing," his mother said firmly.

"Sorry, Cole," Marty said.

"It's okay," Cole assured him. "You go have fun watching your little cousin drool out her birthday candle. I have to work on my green belt test anyway!"

Marty's eyes grew big. "That's right! We've been so busy with the other thing I forgot about that!" He turned back to his mother to plead one last time. "He needs me, Mom, he really needs me!"

But she just shook her head. "He'll have to do without you."

"I'll survive!" Cole said, laughing.

"All right," Marty grumbled. Then he brightened. "I'll see you right after you get it, anyway, since that's when the contest is! Sunday sure is going to be a big day!"

Cole nodded. "Sure is. The biggest." *And the best, I hope*, he added silently.

23

Saturday whizzed by in a blur for Cole. First, he attended karate class, his last as a blue belt if he advanced up a rank the next day. He had no fear of running into Monique then because she always took Saturdays off. Still, he felt a flood of relief when he didn't see her.

After class and a quick lunch, he cornered his mother. "I need a partner to practice my moves on," he said.

"What do I have to do?" she asked.

"You have to attack me," he said.

"I can do that," she said, putting her book aside and jumping to her feet with a grin.

She wasn't grinning an hour later, however. "I had no idea those twisting thingies — What do you call them? Grappling locks? — hurt so much!" she exclaimed as she rubbed her wrists and rotated her shoulders.

"I really appreciate your help, Mom," Cole said gratefully. "And I'm sorry if I hurt you at all."

"No, no, I'm fine!" she insisted. "In fact, I'd be happy to help you out again sometime."

"Maybe you should sign up for lessons yourself!" Cole joked.

He thought she'd laugh it off. But to his surprise, she looked thoughtful.

"You know, maybe I will." She winked. "How do you think I'd look in a gi?" Now she did laugh, seeing his horrified expression. "Never mind!"

Cole worked on other karate material for another hour. Then he rode down the bike path to the brick wall. The letter he'd left wasn't there. But whether Ty had taken it or the wind, he couldn't say. If it was Ty, he'd find out the next day.

Cole slept well that night and awoke in the morning feeling refreshed and ready for the challenges he'd face that day. Marty called to wish him luck with his test.

"I'll see you later, buddy!" he said. "I just hope I recognize you with that flashy new green belt of yours!"

"Let's just hope I'm wearing a flashy new green belt!" Cole countered, suddenly nervous.

"You will," Marty replied. "After all, you've been working with the best — me!"

As Cole laughed, he felt the tension trickle out of him. He thought then how lucky he was to have such a good friend. And if all went well, by the end of the day he'd have earned back another good friend, too.

But first, he had a belt test to take!

The test was scheduled to start at nine o'clock sharp. Cole arrived ten minutes early. Spectators weren't allowed to stay, so his mother gave him a quick hug and left to do errands.

Cole wasn't the only student testing that morning. There were a few orange belts hoping to move up to purple, a handful of yellows looking to jump to orange, and even a few white belts ready to advance to yellow. Of them all, only the white belt kids looked relaxed. In fact, they spent the final minutes before the test charging around after one another.

When Sensei Joe clapped his hands, however, those youngsters and the other students came to attention. Sensei Ann, Sensei Dale, and Sensei Duane were there, too. Sensei Joe bowed them all in and instructed them to put on their belts. Then they bowed again.

With that, it was time for the test to begin.

24

Okay, everybody, line up for basics!" Sensei Joe called.

The students fanned out across the width of the main dojo floor to perform the technique drill.

"Right front stance," Sensei Joe said.

Ten right feet moved in front of ten left feet. "Moving forward with downward blocks," said their instructor. "Ready? Step!"

As one, the students swung their left fists up to their right ears and moved their right fists down in front of their bodies. Then they stepped into a left front stance while whipping their left arms over and down, halting the swing just past their left legs.

"Let's hear some noise out there!" Sensei Joe called. "Step!"

This time, every student punctuated his or her

downward block with a strong cry of *ki-ai*! Step by step, ki-ai by ki-ai, they made their way down the floor. When they could go no farther, they turned to face the other direction.

"Next is a front kick," Sensei Joe told them. He glanced at the little white belt students, some of whom were no older than five. "Don't forget that there are four parts to the kick. Watch."

He demonstrated the move. "Up!" He lifted up his knee so his thigh was parallel with the floor. That was the chamber position.

"Out!" Without moving his upper leg, he swung his foot straight out.

"In!" He pulled the foot back again.

"Down!" Finally, he put his foot down, stepping forward into a front stance as he did.

"Everybody got it?" At their nods, he said, "Then let's go! Step!"

The students kicked their way down the floor. When that move was done, they went on to others: shutos, other blocks and kicks, punches, and strikes.

"Nice job," Sensei Joe said, clapping. "Now we're going to break into separate ranks. White belts, you go with Sensei Ann. Yellow, you're with Sensei Dale.

Sensei Duane will take the oranges, and Cole, you'll come with me. Good luck, everyone. Do your best."

Cole followed Sensei Joe to a spot on the mat. "Let's start with your kumites," the instructor said. Without warning, he threw a straight-in punch right at Cole's head.

Cole didn't have time to think about which of the kumites to do. He just reacted. His right foot took him one angled step forward out of the punch's path. At the same time, his left hand parried the punch away from his face and past his head. His right hand pulled back into firing position — and thrust forward a second later when he twisted toward Sensei Joe and struck with both palms simultaneously, one at his instructor's groin and the other at his jaw.

"He-ya!" he shouted.

Sensei Joe stepped back and nodded. Then he threw a right hook punch.

Cole was expecting the sudden attack this time, but still, he didn't have time to think, just react.

Wham! He blocked the hook with a forceful blow to the inside of Sensei Joe's upper arm. *Slash!* He unleashed a shuto at the man's neck. Then he gripped his sensei's gi collar, sidestepped past his right leg, and

102

wham! drilled his left knee into the back of his thigh, pulling down on the collar as he did. He ended the move with a powerful right punch to the midsection.

None of his strikes had met their targets with full strength. Not that Sensei Joe couldn't handle the hits — he could, and had taken much worse besides, Cole was sure!

On and on the attacks came. Cole messed up his kumites once or twice, but overall he felt he had passed that part of the test — and the grappling maneuvers that followed — without a problem. He silently thanked Marty and his mother for the time they had taken to practice the many moves with him. Without their help, he wasn't sure he would have done them as confidently.

Next came sparring. This was Cole's weakest area and one that he knew he had to work on in the future. But to his relief, he didn't make any of the mistakes he had made when fighting against Monique. Still, he was glad when that section of the test was over!

As he put away his sparring equipment, he noticed that the dojo was almost empty. Only the two orange belts were left, and they were just finishing up the final part of their tests. When they were done, Sensei Joe excused himself to present them with their purple belts and to pose for a few pictures with the happy students. They left soon after, as did Sensei Dale and Sensei Duane.

Now Sensei Joe, Sensei Ann, and Cole were alone in the dojo. A sudden quiet descended over the room. Cole was so used to the training center being filled with laughter, shouts, and other noise that the stillness made him nervous.

Then Sensei Ann laughed at something Sensei Joe said and Cole relaxed. It was a good thing, too, because he still had to perform all his katas for his instructors!

25

Cole stood alone in the middle of the dojo's main floor facing a wall of mirrors. Sensei Joe moved to one side of him, Sensei Ann the other.

"We'll start with Heian One," Sensei Joe said quietly, "and work you up through Two, Three, Four, and Five. Then you'll do your other katas: Taikyoko Five, Yonsu, Wonsu, and Saifa. After that, you'll get your bo staff and perform Bo One and Bo Two for us. Got it?"

Cole nodded. Then he took a deep breath and let it out slowly. Usually, that helped calm his nerves.

This time, it didn't. His heart was pounding. If he made it through all of his katas without faltering, he'd get his green belt, but that was a big if! What if he missed a move, or a transition? What if he didn't put enough power into the punches and blocks? What if he skipped a part by mistake? Just thinking about all the ways he could mess up made his shoulders tense and his back tighten!

Then suddenly, he remembered the underwater kata exercise. His moves then had been slow and controlled. His breathing had been deep and relaxed. Just thinking about it helped him relax now. He closed his eyes once more and took another deep breath. When he opened them, he was ready.

"Ki-ai!" He exploded through Heian One, delivering every block and punch with accuracy and power.

"He-ya!" Each strike, twist, and shuto of Heian Two felt sharp and precise.

As he performed one kata after another, he filled each with more energy and intensity than he ever had before!

When he moved on to his bo forms, he amazed himself with his ability. The slender pole whirled above his head with steady control, stabbed at imaginary targets with ferocity, and whipped over and around his body with ease and grace.

Finally, he came to the end of his last bo kata. Holding the bo horizontal in both hands, he thrust it above his head and then with one hand twirled it beside his body, where it came to rest up along his side. He bowed, making sure the staff didn't come forward with him. Then he straightened and stood stock still, staring at himself in the mirror.

I think I did it, he thought wonderingly. *I really think I did it!*

"You may put your bo away," Sensei Joe said. While Cole hurried across the floor to stow his staff with the other bos, his instructors disappeared into the office.

Cole returned to the floor to stand in ready position. His heart ticked in time with the clock on the wall. He heard the senseis whispering together but he couldn't make out what they were saying. Were they agreeing that he had passed — or discussing where he had failed?

He got his answer a moment later. Both senseis came out of the office and stood before him.

"Cole, step out and remove your belt," Sensei Joe ordered solemnly.

Cole moved his right foot one step sideways and undid the knot of his blue belt. He folded the belt in half, and half again, placed it in his right hand, and resumed his ready stance. His throat was so dry he was sure it would split open if he tried to swallow.

"Step forward," Sensei Joe said.

His voice was so stern that Cole's confidence left him. Any grace he had had during his test fled, too. He nearly stumbled as he moved toward his senseis.

Then he looked up and saw that Sensei Joe was smiling.

His instructor reached into his gi top and pulled out a crisp, clean green belt. "Congratulations, Cole," he said, his smile broadening into a grin. "Very well done!"

He took Cole's old blue belt from him, presented him with the new belt, shook his hand, and bowed.

Cole gripped his new belt tightly and burst into a happy laugh. "Woohoo!" he shouted. "I did it!"

To his surprise, his shout was echoed by others. He whirled around to face the waiting room. There stood his mother, Marty, Marty's mother — and Ty!

"Yes!" Cole yelled, pumping his fist and pointing at the teenager. "You got my letter!"

Ty didn't answer. He just held up a wrinkled envelope and grinned.

26

Is that who I think it is?"

Cole turned back to see Sensei Joe staring at Ty with a puzzled expression.

"Ty? Ty Matthewson?" his instructor said. "It is you, isn't it!"

Ty's smile turned hesitant, but he nodded.

"Well, get in here, son," Sensei Joe cried, "and tell me what the heck you've been up to all these years!"

Ty did as his former instructor asked. He and Sensei Joe stood together in the dojo, talking animatedly. Cole watched them with satisfaction. Something told him that Ty would be returning to karate soon!

"Way to go, buddy!" Marty grabbed Cole in a big bear hug. "I knew you could do it!"

"Thanks, Marty — for everything," Cole said. He

held up his green belt. "I couldn't have gotten this without your help."

"So you'll return the favor when it's my turn," Marty said. "After all, I may be testing soon myself!"

Cole's mother came in next. She took Cole's old blue belt from Sensei Joe and then turned to her son, beaming. "We sneaked in during the last minutes of your test," she confessed. "You looked so strong and confident out there, Cole! I'm so proud of you!"

"Thanks, Mom. Hi, Mrs. Bronson. Thanks for coming!"

Marty's mother smiled at him. "I look forward to seeing Marty in your shoes — or rather, bare feet — in a few months. Now what do you say we all go and get some lunch before the kata contest?"

"Marty and I have something to talk to Sensei Joe about first," Cole said, giving Marty a significant look. Their mothers sat down to chat.

"What is it, boys?" Sensei Joe asked when he saw Cole and Marty waiting for him to finish talking with Ty.

"It's about the kata contest," Cole said. "We were hoping to get your permission to do something a little . . . special."

"Come into my office and explain what you have in mind," Sensei Joe said. Then he shook Ty's hand, saying, "Stop by after school tomorrow and we'll see about getting you a new gi. Something tells me you've outgrown your old one!"

Ty laughed. Then, as he turned to leave, he slapped Cole on the back. "Sure am glad I met you," he said. "See you at the contest."

"Now, boys, what is it you wanted to ask me?" Sensei Joe said.

"Well, sir, it's like this . . ."

Ten minutes later, Cole and Marty had their instructor's permission to do what they hoped to do. "Cross your fingers that this works," Cole said as they joined their mothers in the waiting area. "If not, I'm afraid I'll have lost a friend I just found again."

The kata contest was being held at two o'clock that afternoon. Cole, Marty, and their mothers returned to the dojo at 1:45 PM. Other karate students and their families were there, including Monique and her parents. She glanced at Cole when he walked in but then quickly looked away.

At two o'clock sharp, Sensei Joe came out of his

111

office and asked everyone to please gather in the main dojo. "I'm sorry I don't have enough chairs for everyone," he said. "But go ahead and grab some floor!"

When everyone was settled, he explained what the contest was all about. "At our dojo, we teach century-old techniques and moves. We also work to build character, increase confidence, and encourage students to respect themselves and others. This contest taps into all these things. After all, contestants are testing their karate knowledge by creating their own katas. They're also displaying confidence and strength of character by entering the contest. Many of them talked over ideas with others, a sign that they trust that their concepts would be greeted with respect."

He smiled then. "But most of all, we decided to run this contest because, well, we thought the kids would have fun making up their own katas! So, without further ado, let's get to it!"

He consulted a clipboard. "First up is Melissa Darlington. Come on up, Melissa, and let's see what you created."

Melissa was a yellow belt. She hadn't been training for long, so she didn't have a wide range of moves. But she did a nice job with a series of upward blocks, straight-in punches, and a few kicks. The audience applauded her efforts appreciatively.

Next up was Dan, one of the students who had just tested that morning. He wore his new purple belt with pride. Unfortunately, he seemed to forget how his own kata went, for after six moves, he just stopped, bowed, and sat down with a sheepish look on his face.

"All right, Dan, no problem," Sensei Joe reassured. "When we run the contest next time, you can show us the whole thing!"

A blue belt went next, and then an orange belt. Both had put together nice katas, Cole thought. But in his opinion, the winner hadn't yet performed.

Then Sensei Joe called out the next name. "Monique Cleary, you're up!" As she rose to her feet, however, he held up a hand. "But first, let's take a short break. Five minutes, folks, and then we'll be back!"

Cole and Marty exchanged looks. They got to their feet and, moving as stealthily as cats on the prowl, disappeared into the storage room.

"Did she see us?" Marty whispered.

"I don't think so," Cole replied. "Now we just have to wait for the right moment."

27

Five minutes passed. Cole could tell when the audience had resumed their seats because everything got quiet. He waited a beat longer and then whispered, "Ready?"

Marty nodded, opened the storage room door, and tiptoed out with Cole at his heels.

Monique stood in ready position before the audience. Her eyes were focused forward. Her back was to the boys.

As quietly as they could, Cole and Marty moved to stand behind and on either side of her. Several of the people in the audience whispered and pointed at them. Cole lifted a finger to his lips to plead for their silence.

"Whenever you're ready, Monique," Sensei Joe encouraged.

She nodded once. Then she took a deep breath and bowed.

Behind her, Cole and Marty bowed, too. And when she began her kata, they did as well.

Upward block! Palm heel strike! She had no idea that they were behind her until — "Ki-ai!" — her own cry was joined by those of the boys!

She froze. For a split second, Cole thought she would stop altogether. But she didn't. She turned into her next move, her fists one over the other, and then stepped forward for the low straight-in punch followed by the kick.

Marty and Cole did each move with her in perfect unison.

"He-ya!" the three shouted together.

Around they turned to the opposite direction, to do the cross shuto, the knee, and the double punch.

"Ki-ai!"

Then came the throw, a sweeping move that saw both arms circling up, over, and around, ending with the fingers pointing to the ground. The throw turned them to the back of the room. That's where they directed their right straight-in punches and left snap kicks.

"He-ya!"

Back around they spun, three-quarters to the right, for another cross-shuto, this one with the opposite hand. Knee and punch came after and then —

"Ki-ai!"

— another three-quarter spin into an outward elbow jab found them facing the audience again. But only for a second, for with the next move, a left circular outward block, they shifted to the left. A spear and a punch — "Ki-ai!" — finished the kata.

As one, they turned to the front, crossed their fists in front of them, and bowed.

There was silence for a heartbeat. Then the audience exploded with applause and whistles. Sensei Joe stepped forward, clapping and smiling. "I think we have a winner," he said, and the crowd roared with approval.

Monique hadn't moved. Cole walked toward her, unsure if she was happy or furious. Then she turned and looked at him. Her blue eyes were shining and she was smiling from one ear to the other.

"You learned my kata!" she said. "I can't believe it!"

Cole stabbed his toe at the wood floor. "I had to do something to make up for what I did," he said. "I'm really, *really* sorry for taking it out of your bag."

Monique's smile faded. "It was a rotten thing to do," she said.

"I know," he admitted. "And I don't mean to make excuses but . . . why didn't you tell me and Marty that you had made up a kata? Why did you make it sound like you weren't going to enter the contest?"

She turned away but not before he saw her blush. "I *wasn't* sure if was going to enter, because I wasn't sure if my kata was any good. That's why I didn't show it to you, either. I thought you might laugh or call it dumb or something."

Cole was about to protest that he'd never do anything like that. Then he thought back to how he had often treated her and realized she had every reason to think that he might. He heaved a big sigh.

"I might be a green belt," he said then, "but I think maybe I need to return to white belt level. Seems I've forgotten the part of my training that teaches me how to respect others and be a good person."

Monique threw an arm around his shoulder. "Aw, don't worry, we all make mistakes sometimes. And —"

She stopped talking suddenly. Cole looked up to see her staring through into the waiting room at a person standing there. It was Ty. He was staring right back at her. Both wore amazed expressions.

"I know him," she said. "He's the boy who tried to help me and my mother in the playground all those years ago!"

"You started taking private lessons right after that, didn't you?" Cole asked.

"Yes!" she exclaimed in astonishment. "How did you —?"

Cole punched her lightly in the ribs. "Come on, let's go see him. And I'll tell you all about how I figured out one of the greatest mysteries of my life."

"Which is?"

"Why you started taking private lessons — and why I didn't do the same thing when you jumped ahead of me in rank!" He laughed out loud. "Just think! If I had, you and I would be even, and I wouldn't have spent the last three-and-a-half years being jealous of you. Instead, we could have stayed friends."

She returned his punch with one of her own. "Well, we're friends again now."

"That's right," Cole agreed just as Marty came up and looped his arms across their shoulders. "And that's how I intend to keep it from now on!"

Matt Christopher®

Muhammad Ali

Lance Armstrong

Kobe Bryant

Jennifer Capriati

Dale Earnhardt Sr.

Jeff Gordon

Ken Griffey Jr.

Mia Hamm

Tony Hawk

Ichiro

LeBron James

Derek Jeter

Randy Johnson

Michael Jordan

Peyton and Eli Manning

Yao Ming

Shaquille O'Neal

Albert Pujols

Jackie Robinson

Alex Rodriguez

Babe Ruth

Curt Schilling

Sammy Sosa

Tiger Woods

All available in paperback from Little, Brown and Company
**Previously published as Pressure Play
***Previously published as Baseball Pals